My First Phanatic Book

by Eli Kowalski

Meet the Phillie Phanatic

Phanatic Phun Phacts:

BIRTHPLACE: Galapagos Islands

PHYSICAL ATTRIBUTES: Overweight, clumsy feet, extra-long beak, curled up tongue, gawking neck, ("slight" case of body odor.)

MOM: Phoebe

BEST FRIEND: Phyllis

FAVORITE FOODS: Soft pretzels, Scrapple, hoagies, cheesesteaks and Tastykakes

FAVORITE MOVIE: Rocky

FAVORITE SONG: *Motownphilly* by Boyz II Men and *Take Me Out To The Ballgame.*

MOST MEMORABLE MOMENT: Riding down Broad Street in the 1980 World Series and the 2008 World Series Championship Parades.

4

THE PHANATIC MEASURES:

Height:
6'5"

Waistline:
90"

Weight:
300 lbs.

Shoe size:
20

The Phanatic lives at Citizens Bank Park, home of the Philadelphia Phillies.

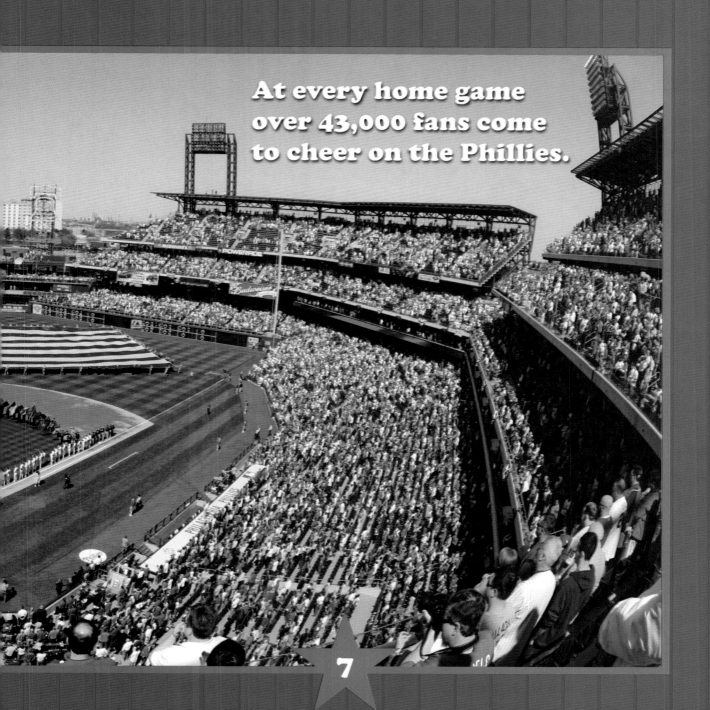

At every home game over 43,000 fans come to cheer on the Phillies.

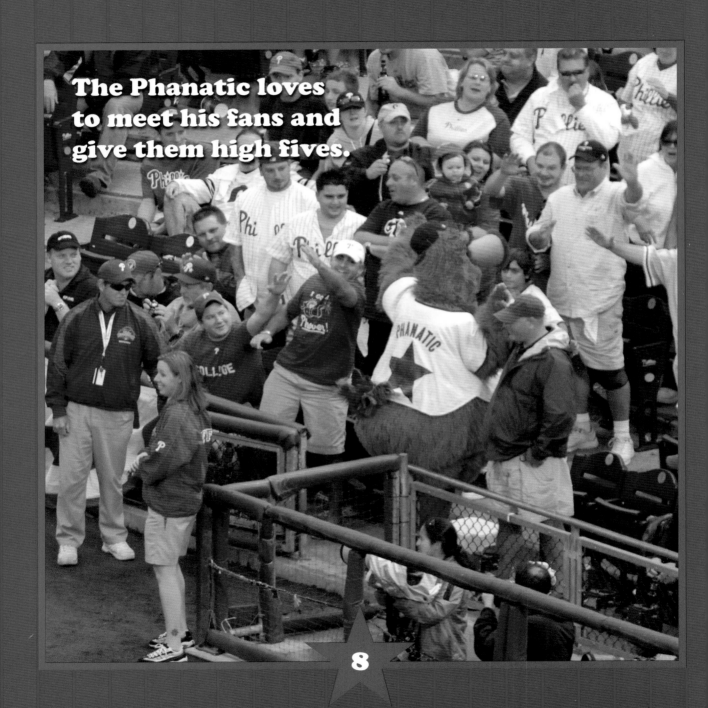

The Phanatic loves to meet his fans and give them high fives.

8

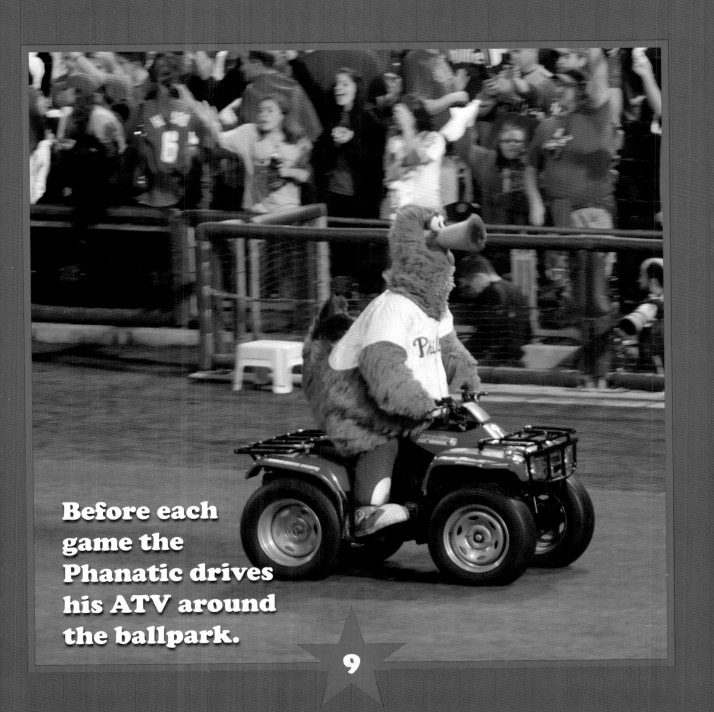

Before each game the Phanatic drives his ATV around the ballpark.

Sometimes he drives
sitting down.

10

Sometimes the Phanatic drives standing up!

Sometimes Lady Pha Pha makes an appearance . . .

12

. . . or even one of the "Blue Guys" takes the ATV for a ride.

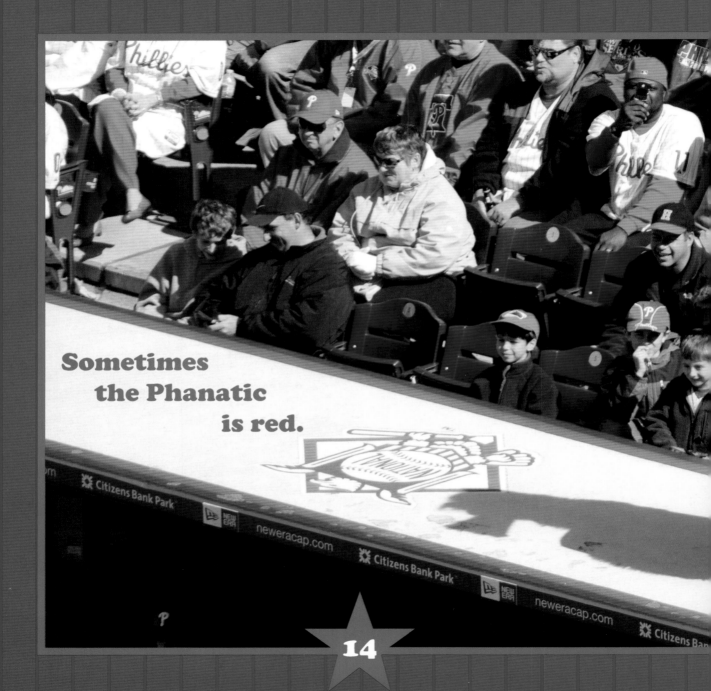

Sometimes
the Phanatic
is red.

The Phanatic
LOVES to
dress up . . .

PHILLIES

16

. . . and shake
his hips.

The Phanatic sometimes loses his jersey.

Uh Oh!

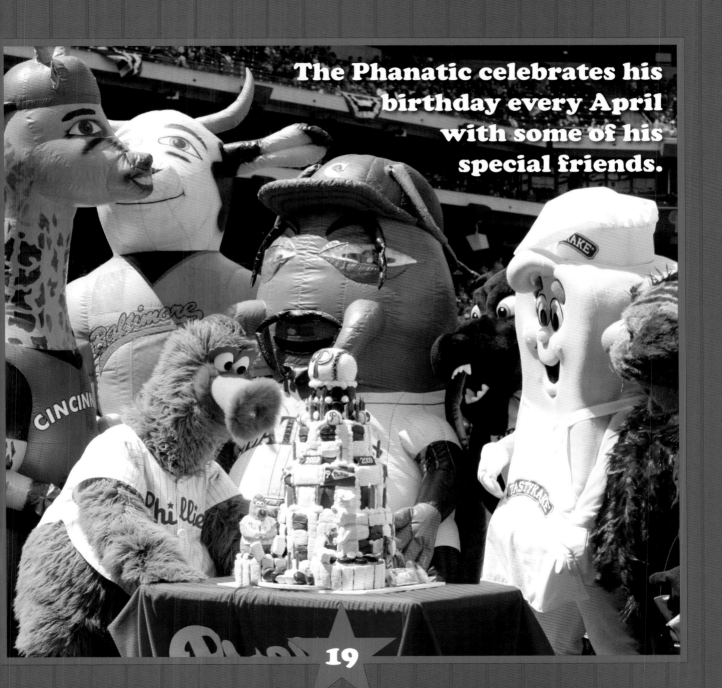

The Phanatic celebrates his birthday every April with some of his special friends.

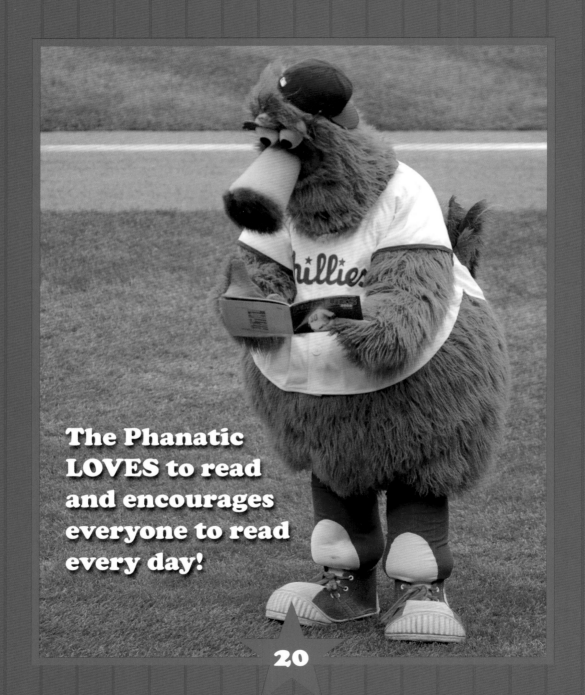

The Phanatic
LOVES to read
and encourages
everyone to read
every day!

20

The Phanatic also enjoys dancing and entertaining the fans on top of the Phillies dugout.

It could be with the turtles . . .

. . . or it could be with his best friend Phyllis.

neweracap.com Citizens Bank Park

23

You just never know which of the fans the Phanatic is going to invite to dance with him.

He sometimes gets so excited a lucky fan gets a shower of popcorn.

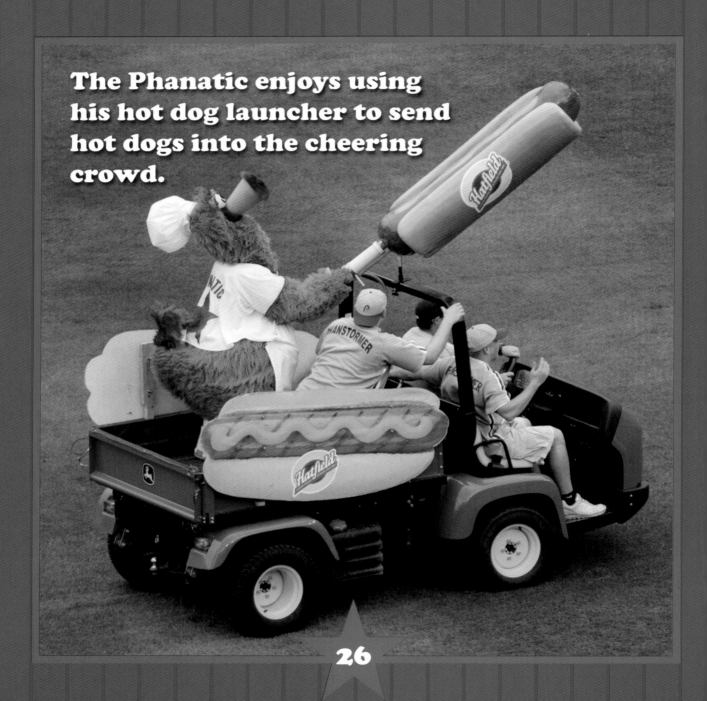

The Phanatic enjoys using his hot dog launcher to send hot dogs into the cheering crowd.

The Phanatic tries to put a "whammy" on the other teams' batters.

27

Now let's all join in singing . . .

28

Bank Park™   neweracap.co   Citizens Bank Park™

Take Me Out to the Ballgame:

"Take me out to the ball game,

Take me out with the crowd.

Buy me some peanuts and
cracker jack,

I don't care if I never get back,

Let me root, root, root for the Phillies,

If they don't win it's a shame.

For it's one, two, three strikes,
you're out,

At the old ball game."

The Phanatic is always ready to party . . .

. . . especially during the Phillies Post Season.

31

The Phanatic was so proud holding the World Series trophy. He wanted everyone to see it.

Let's go
PHILLIES!